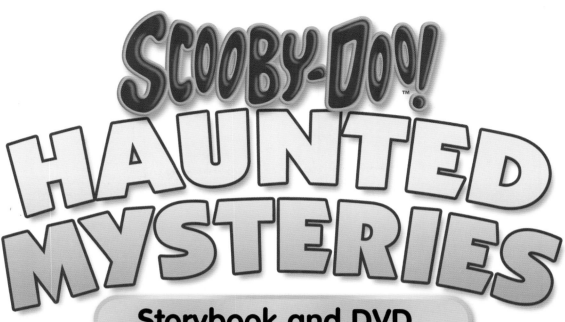

SCOOBY-DOO!
HAUNTED MYSTERIES

Storybook and DVD

adapted by Justine Fontes
illustrated by MADA Design

The Haunted House Hang-up 6

Go Away, Ghost Ship! 14

What the Hex Is Going On? 22

A Night of Fright Is No Delight 30

Reader's
Digest
Children's Books®

Pleasantville, New York • Montréal, Québec • Bath, United Kingdom

The Haunted House Hang-up

S cooby-Doo, Shaggy, and the gang were on their way
to a rock concert, when their van suddenly overheated.
Now they were just where they didn't want to be—parked in front
of a spooky mansion! Earlier, a scary-looking man named Asa
Shanks had warned the teens to stay away from the mansion. He
said it was haunted. But the gang needed water for the van, and
there was a well next to the mansion, so what else could they do?

When Shaggy turned the well's crank, something moaned!

"Rikes!" barked Scooby-Doo. Then a white ghost rose from the well.

"Triple yikes!" shouted Shaggy.

Daphne saw a light inside the mansion. That meant someone was
home. So the friends went inside to ask for a bucket of water.

Inside the mansion, the kids saw a peculiar-looking portrait. Shaggy read the name plaque. It read: Jefferson Stillwall.

"He must have owned this place once. I wonder what he's pointing at?" Shaggy said.

Creak! Squeak! Shaggy looked around. The whole gang was right in front of him. So who could be walking around outside the door?

The kids opened the door to investigate. It was dark, so Shaggy grabbed Velma's hand—except it wasn't Velma's hand at all. The cold, clammy hand belonged to none other than the Headless Specter! Shaggy shuddered. Asa Shanks had said no one who saw the Headless Specter lived to tell about it. What if he was right?

The Headless Specter
began to chase Shaggy, Velma,
and Scooby. They ran outside. Since it was dark, they didn't see
the well. Shaggy, Scooby, and Velma all ended up falling into it.

"Help! I'm drowning!" Shaggy's voice echoed in the dark,
deep hole.

Scooby-Doo laughed. The water wasn't even knee deep!
As Velma leaned on the well wall,
suddenly a secret door opened.
It led to the cellar of the
mansion, where they found
Fred and Daphne examining
a bunch of helium canisters
and huge balloons.

Daphne and Fred also found an old diary. The last entry read, "Marching men in single file hide the secret. Stillwall shows the way." The gang guessed that meant the man in the portrait was pointing to something important.

"A line of men could mean a column," Velma said. "Find the column Stillwall's pointing at, and we'll solve this mystery!"

The painted finger pointed to the greenhouse. But there were no columns near the greenhouse.

Suddenly, the Headless Specter appeared again! Shaggy wanted to get away fast, but how? He remembered the balloons and helium canisters. He and Scooby ran to the cellar, the Specter at their heels. They quickly filled balloons and jumped on them. It might have been fun flying along on the balloons—if the Headless Specter hadn't jumped on his own balloon to follow them.

They raced along until they all crashed into the chicken shed. The impact also revealed who the Headless Specter was. A head popped out of his collar, revealing that the Specter was Penrod Stillwall, the great, great, great grandson of Jefferson Stillwall. "I tried to scare people away so they wouldn't steal my great, great, great grandfather's treasure," he explained. "It's hidden someplace around here."

"We'll help you find it!" Velma volunteered.

Then they all heard banging noises, like an ax chopping wood. Shaggy looked up and said, "Sounds like a ghost in the attic."

"Let's go flush him out!" Fred exclaimed.

Shaggy wanted to run away, but instead, Fred convinced him to lead the ghost into a trap! Shaggy would lead the ghost out the front door, where Velma and Daphne would trip up the ghost with a rope across the threshold.

"Get ready! He's right behind us," Fred called to the girls. As soon as the ghost crossed the threshold, Daphne and Velma pulled their rope tight. *THUMP!* The ghost tripped, then crashed into a column, causing it to break into pieces on the porch. A familiar face poked out from beneath a white sheet with eyeholes cut in it. Stillwall exclaimed, "It's my greedy neighbor, Asa Shanks, trying to steal my treasure!"

"And I'd have found it, if not for you young people," Asa grumbled as he was led away.

To solve the mystery and find where the treasure was hidden, watch the DVD, study the clues, and solve the mystery.

Go Away, Ghost Ship!

"Red Beard the pirate swore revenge on my ancestors," Mr. Magnus told the Mystery, Inc. teens. Even though Red Beard was long dead, Magnus, a shipping company owner, blamed the pirate's ghost for stealing his freighters in a mysterious fog.

Velma was skeptical. How could a dead pirate still steal?

The gang decided to test Mr. Magnus' theory with "Operation Decoy." They put a foghorn on a rowboat to make it sound like a freighter.

But the trick worked too well! Moments later, a ghostly pirate ship was heading straight for them. Fred shouted, "Full speed reverse!"

"Like double reverse," Shaggy agreed.

The pirate ship came closer and closer. Then *SMASH!* The rowboat was rammed to pieces! Scooby-Doo and all his friends were up to their necks in sea water. "Oh, my hairdo!" Daphne cried.

There was no place to go except the pirate ship, so the gang scrambled aboard. In the soggy and foggy confusion, Shaggy and Scooby-Doo got separated from the others.

Fred, Velma, and Daphne searched the spooky ship for their friends. In the hold, they expected to find cargo. Instead, there were tubs of dry ice.

"Why would ghosts need dry ice?" Fred wondered.

CLICK! The door shut behind them.

"We're locked in!" Velma exclaimed.

Then they heard ghostly laughter. Who was laughing and why?

On the other side of the thick door, Shaggy saw a painting of a pirate come to life right before his eyes. "Zoinks! It's Red Beard!" Shaggy shouted.

Suddenly, swords started floating through the air! Scooby-Doo and Shaggy ran into a cabin and slammed the door. A sword hit the door with a loud *THUNK!*

The door crashed open and three pirates now stood there. Shaggy counted them on his shaking fingers. "One, two, three ghosts!" Shaggy and Scooby-Doo sank to the floor, faint with fear.

Shaggy looked up at Captain Red Beard and cringed. "What are you going to do with us, your ghostliness?"

As soon as they could, Shaggy and Scooby-Doo escaped from Red Beard. But how would they get his two henchmen off their heels?

Shaggy looked around. He saw a big piece of paper full of lists and numbers. He folded it into a pirate hat. Now his shadow looked just like Red Beard's. Shaggy pointed his finger from his hiding place. He imitated Red Beard's voice and ordered the two henchmen, "Get going! They went that way, you swabs."

The henchmen obediently ran the other way. Scooby-Doo chuckled quietly.

Of course, that didn't fool the "real" Red Beard! When the pirate caught up with Shaggy and Scooby, he was angrier than ever.

Red Beard chased them all over the ship. Finally, Scooby and Shaggy made their escape by frantically rowing a wooden barrel to shore. They found themselves at a mysterious warehouse along a lonely cove. The rest of the Mystery, Inc. gang was already there. The warehouse was full of crates. This had to be the stuff stolen from Mr. Magnus' ships. *WHOOSH!* A sword suddenly flew through the air.

"Zoinks!" Shaggy shouted. "It's the blade again." Then they noticed Red Beard's two henchmen had appeared again.

Shaggy and Scooby scrambled into a crate. It smelled wonderful. They looked down and saw boxes and boxes of…Scooby Snacks!

"Re-licious!" Scooby-Doo cried.

But who had time to eat? The gang searched frantically through the crates for weapons. They found archery bows and toilet plungers.

"Make your shots count," Fred said.

Velma took careful aim. "Bull's-eye!" she said, as she shot one of Red Beard's henchmen with a plunger.

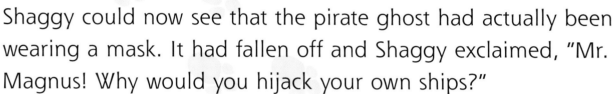

Shaggy and Scooby grabbed a jackhammer and rode it like a pogo stick. The jackhammer got caught in Red Beard's belt, and the ghost pirate bounced his way right into a pile of tires. Shaggy could now see that the pirate ghost had actually been wearing a mask. It had fallen off and Shaggy exclaimed, "Mr. Magnus! Why would you hijack your own ships?"

To find out why Mr. Magnus was hijacking his own ships, watch the DVD, study the clues, and find out what really was going on.

What the Hex Is Going On?

"An eerie voice called me to the old Kingston Mansion. I had to obey," recalled Sharon Wetherby's Uncle Stewart. "In the mansion, I saw the ghost of Elias Kingston."

Scooby and Shaggy shivered. What happened to their fun country weekend full of food, food, and more food? Sharon and her father looked worried—and Uncle Stewart suddenly looked about a hundred years old!

Stewart went on with his story. "The ghost said, 'the Wetherby fortune belongs to me. Return it or the entire family will suffer this terrible fate.'" And then, in an instant, Elias Kingston had turned him into an old man!

Mr. Wetherby tried to call the police, but the phone was dead. The gang promised to investigate while Mr. Wetherby drove to town to get the sheriff.

Scooby was assigned to be the watchdog, but he fell asleep on guard duty. When he woke up, both Uncle Stewart and Sharon were gone! The team rushed to the Kingston Mansion to see if they were there.

While the others looked for Sharon and her uncle, Scooby searched for a snack. He found a bone in the refrigerator. But the bone belonged to an angry guard dog.

Suddenly, the ghost of Elias Kingston appeared. He issued a final warning: If he didn't get the fortune by morning, every Wetherby would be turned into an old man or woman. The gang followed the

ghost to the mausoleum, where they found fingerprints on the door and a strange book inside.

The book title was *Crystalomacy*.

"That's how to use a fortune-teller's crystal ball," Daphne said.

Fred replied, "Maybe there's a connection to that fortune-teller's place in town."

Then the door slammed shut. They were trapped in the dark creepy crypt!

"Tap the walls," Fred said. The gang knew a secret passage would make a wall sound hollow. Sure enough, Scooby found a wall that spun around. Behind it was a dark tunnel.

The passage led back to the Wetherby estate. From there, the gang raced to the fortune-teller's shop. No one was home, so they decided to have a look around. Shaggy saw someone's face inside the crystal ball.

Shaggy exclaimed, "Zoinks! It's the ghost of Elias Kingston!"

"You didn't do as I said. Now you will pay!" shouted the head of Elias Kingston.

Suddenly, the table holding the crystal ball floated right off the floor! "That table's out to get us!" Velma cried, as the table scooted toward the teens.

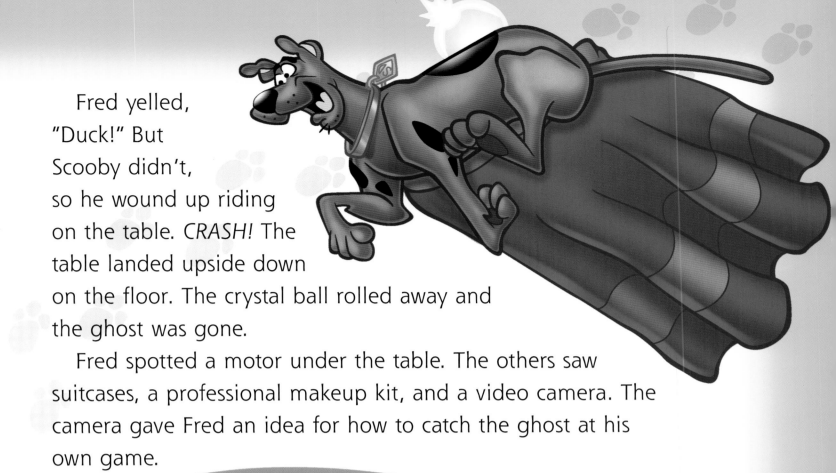

Fred yelled,
"Duck!" But
Scooby didn't,
so he wound up riding
on the table. *CRASH!* The
table landed upside down
on the floor. The crystal ball rolled away and
the ghost was gone.

Fred spotted a motor under the table. The others saw
suitcases, a professional makeup kit, and a video camera. The
camera gave Fred an idea for how to catch the ghost at his
own game.

Shaggy and Scooby brought an empty treasure chest back to the mansion.

Elias Kingston was pleased.

"You brought the fortune. How fortunate for you," he said. But when the ghost opened the box, a toy clown squirted him with water! As Fred hoped, the furious ghost chased Shaggy and Scooby right into a trap.

Suddenly, the ghost saw two other ghosts that looked exactly like him. He didn't know Fred had rigged up the video camera to capture the ghost's image and then projected two fake ghosts into the room.

"This place is really haunted!" the ghost exclaimed. Then he saw a giant image of Scooby-Doo and ran straight into the gang's net.

Daphne chuckled, "Golly, he's running like a ghost is after him."

When the ghost was tied up, Fred explained to Mr. Wetherby, "This ghost doesn't really need an introduction. As soon as he's cleaned up, you'll recognize him."

Sharon exclaimed, "Uncle Stewart! Why on earth would you pretend to be a ghost?"

To find out why Uncle Stewart was pretending to be a ghost, watch the DVD, study the clues, and solve the mystery.

The last place Scooby-Doo wanted to be was in another spooky old mansion. But how could he pass up a chance to inherit a fortune? Colonel Beauregard Saunders' money would buy a lot of Scooby Snacks! Years ago, Scooby had rescued the colonel, and in gratitude, Scooby had been included in his will.

When all the colonel's relatives and Scooby were settled in their chairs, the lawyer introduced himself. "I am Carsgood Creeps. My partner, Mr. Crawls, regrets that he could not be here with us." Then Mr. Creeps played a tape of Beauregard Saunders reading his own will.

"Greetings, y'all..." the recording began. Then the colonel said they would all get an equal share of his fortune if "you spend tonight in the old family mansion."

Mr. Creeps shut off the tape and reminded them that anyone who left the mansion would be cut out of the will. Then he said with a smirk, "Pleasant dreams, y'all."

After the lawyer left, strange things started happening. At midnight, two ghost-like creatures crept into Cousin Simple's room. By the time the others arrived, all they found was Simple's nightcap and a poem written on the mirror:

This first is gone, the rest will go, unless you leave the island and row, row, row.
—The Shadow Phantom

In a secret passage under the mansion, the teens found footprints. Velma wondered out loud, "Why would a Shadow Phantom leave footprints?"

"Dirty feet?" Shaggy suggested. Shaggy tried to run away, but Velma stopped him.

"You're going to be brave no matter how chicken you are." So they kept exploring the spooky mansion.

Shaggy found a collection of Civil War clothes and uniforms.
One uniform suddenly stood up and began to chase him! Shaggy
shouted, "Zoinks! Haunted uniforms!"

When the uniform cornered Scooby-Doo, he
growled and made scary faces. A frightened goose
waddled out of the jacket.

Meanwhile, thanks to the Shadow Phantom,
four more heirs vanished. At this rate, there
would be no one left to inherit the colonel's
fortune—except Scooby-Doo.

Then two green ghosts suddenly appeared! What could Scooby do? He and Shaggy disguised themselves in Civil War clothes. Then they danced the ghosts over an open trap door, and dropped them into it. When Shaggy looked at his hand, there was green stuff all over it.

Whoever heard of ghosts leaving traces of makeup or paint? Now the gang was even more convinced that real ghosts weren't haunting the mansion, so they set an elaborate trap made from an old washing machine.

Pretty soon the villains were "all washed up." The "ghosts" turned out to be Mr. Creeps and his partner, Mr. Crawls. The gang wondered, had the lawyers been trying to scare the heirs away from the colonel's mansion so they could keep the fortune for themselves? If so, they might have succeeded had it not been for the clever teenagers of Mystery, Inc. and their furry friend, Scooby-Doo!

To find out what happened, and who ended up inheriting the fortune, watch the DVD, study the clues, and solve the mystery.